Hannah Finds Her Voice

written by Robin Conrad Sturm
illustrated by Stacey Jackson

Hannah Finds Her Voice

Copyright © 2016 Robin Conrad Sturm

Publisher's Note: This is a work of fiction.

Ordering Information: Special discounts are available on quantity purchases by schools, corporations, associations, and others. For details, contact the publisher at rob2stu@aol.com.

Robin Conrad Sturm — First Edition

ISBN 978-1-935355-18-2

Printed in the United States of America

This book is dedicated to "the pure in heart, for they shall see God."

Acknowledgements

I would like to thank all of my students, who are constant sources of inspiration and perseverance. Being a teacher means I never have to stop learning; there will always be someone and something different every year to teach me something new.

A little girl named Hannah sat on her bed one day;
She looked outside the window watching other children play.
She watched them running, jumping high, around and 'round they'd run
She tapped the glass and waved hello to join in on the fun.
But no one looked or smiled back, Hannah didn't understand;
She loved to laugh and hug her friends, but they had other plans.

Hannah always struggled to run and keep up with her friends;
She didn't understand their jokes; she couldn't talk like them.
She had so many things to say about her days at school.
Perhaps a joke, or song she'd heard, but children can be cruel.
She felt she had no voice, her friends just didn't know her plight.
It was so hard to form her words; she couldn't get them right.

Kids grew impatient, so they wouldn't give her time to speak -
Hannah felt so lonely, every day, week after week.
She didn't know why Mom and Dad would stay close by her side;
The other kids could walk to school, they freely roamed outside.
But Hannah took a different bus, her friends would wave good-bye -
She struggled hard to hide her tears, she always wondered why.

She had so many things to say, to do, to make believe!
She made up stories, pets and friends to make her day complete.
One time she heard her momma talk while she was on the phone;
She heard a word she'd never learned; it had a somber tone.
The word was "Downs," it made her think, "Are they talking about me?"
So Mom held Hannah close as Hannah sat upon her knee.

When Hannah went to school each day she worked so very hard!
Although she loved her teacher, she would gaze into the yard-
She watched the clouds change shape, she watched the trees sway in the wind,
The flowers fluttered back and forth, they giggled on their stems!
Back home again she'd run outside alone to join their dance.
They seemed to speak a different way; to Hannah, they made sense!

One day in school, a special treat filled Hannah's heart with joy -
A group of dancers came to entertain the girls and boys!
They jumped and twirled and filled the stage, and Hannah's heart just leaped!
She saw they could communicate and never have to speak!
A fire was lit in Hannah's heart, somehow she always knew
There had to be a way that she could silently "speak" too!

So Hannah burst into the house when she got home that day;
She tried to tell her mom and dad; it was *so* hard to say!
But she kept trying, so her mom picked up the phone to call;
The teacher told her everything, how Hannah was in awe!
So Mom began the daunting job to find a ballet school
Who'd love her very precious child and teach her little jewel.

Though Hannah still was very young, she had some grown up dreams:
She longed to be expressive and to dance just like those trees.
She wanted to tell stories and to shout her feelings loud,
To "giggle" like those flowers, or to float just like those clouds!
So off to ballet class she went, her hand was held so tight,
But then she saw the great big room with mirrors shining bright!

Into the studio she ran, around the room she raced!
She jumped and spun and clapped her hands; her joy was on her face.
The teacher walked into the room- time for the class to start!
But Hannah didn't want to stop; the happiness filled her heart.
Then all the students gathered 'round; the teacher had to say
That learning to dance is hard, hard work; it's not the time to play!

The teacher made them twist and bend, and then reach very tall!
Standing still was *very* hard, she could *not* do that at all!
The others learned so very fast, and Hannah tried her best.
She seemed to stumble all the time while the others twirled right past!
Still Hannah loved her teacher and the other students, too.
So every week, year after year, she went to ballet school.

Hannah was having so much fun; her parents were so proud,
But when the others moved up a class, Hannah was not allowed.
Although she worked and worked and worked, it never seemed enough
To move up to the higher class. To stay behind was rough.
Hannah learned that ballet school was harder than she thought.
But all the while she picked up seeds that grew inside her heart.

Hannah never gave up hope; she worked all through the years.
She always worked so hard, whether with laughter or through tears.
Hannah truly loved to dance, it always felt like play-
But slowly she was learning how to speak another way!
She danced when she was happy, or alone or so upset;
The movements she had learned were actually an alphabet!

The years, at first, crept slowly by, but then, before she knew,
Hannah was a senior and her school days were through.
Although this day seemed so far off when everything began,
Her teachers always taught her not to give up on her plans.
But Hannah had a secret which she didn't dare to dream,
A dream that started many years ago as just a seed:

At ballet school the seniors danced a solo every year.
The solo signified their growth throughout their school career.
Hannah watched them every year, but she was too afraid
To think that she would be allowed that moment on the stage.
But Hannah didn't realize just how much she had learned.
She had a way to speak her heart, and now it was her turn!

So every week she worked with Ballet Teacher on a dance.
They practiced how to use her art to touch an audience.
Sometimes she would forget the steps they did the week before,
But every week, her speaking through her dance grew even more.
The more she tried, the smiles came, her confidence was showing.
The joy she felt was bubbling up! Her dancing words were growing!

The time had come to think about the costume she would wear!
It had to be a color and style to show off Hannah's flair.
Purple and pink made Hannah smile, so to the store they went
To find the fabric for her dress that told her story best.
Mom and Hannah found the cloth! The sewing could begin
To make Hannah feel more beautiful than she had ever been!

The time flew by, she knew her dance, the costume now was done;
The sparkling, flowing fabric seemed to dance all on its own!
When Hannah tried it on, Mom knew that this would always be
The moment she'd remember most: to see her daughter beam!
Hannah jumped and twirled around, the mirror showed her face -
The shiny smile that used to fade was firmly now in place!

The day was here! As Hannah woke, she felt a little scared.
Although her legs knew what to do, her heart felt unprepared.
Her costume and her ballet bag were set out by the door;
She didn't know if she had ever been this scared before!
Her mom and dad fled through their day; they had *so* much to do!
But Hannah thought about tonight; her fear just grew and grew.

And then she thought back to the time when she was very small
And saw those dancers at her school who filled her heart with awe.
They seemed to move so easily; they spoke through every move.
And from that moment, Hannah knew she had to do that too!
Her years of training gave her all the confidence she'd need
To take her moment on that stage- her heart had now been freed.

The waiting now was over, Mom and Dad exclaimed, "Let's go!"
With eager smiles replacing doubt, she rode off to the show.
All the dancers milled about as Hannah reached the door.
Excitement pushed away the fears that plagued her thoughts before.
The dancers found their dressing rooms while families found their seats,
But Hannah's mom stayed by her side to meet her daughter's needs.

Hannah was now ready, make up on, hair in a bun-
The tights and leotard were on, the warm up was all done.
A final kiss from Mom before she left to find her seat,
And Hannah turned to face the stage; preparations were complete.
The long awaited time was here, and Hannah held on tight
To all her dreams wrapped up in this one piece she'd dance tonight!

"Dancers, onstage!" Hannah heard the Ballet Teacher call!
As each class took their turn to dance, the audience was enthralled!
Hannah almost held her breath as she prepared to dance,
She watched each class before her, knowing soon would come her chance.
From youngest to the oldest, all that training had been spent
To make this day so special - a most memorable event!

Now all the class pieces were done, and Hannah ran to dress
Into the costume she had dreamed about and had caressed.
Her hair was done, the costume on, she checked the mirror twice.
She saw the sparkles on her dress, but more were in her eyes!
Then Hannah ran backstage to prepare her dance and take her place.
She heard Ballet Teacher call her name; a smile lit her face.

Hannah heard the music start, she stepped out on the stage.
The lights shone brightly in her eyes, yet she was not afraid.
The time for fear was now long gone, her joy had filled her heart;
She's had a story to tell the world, *now* was the time to start.
With every movement, Hannah's hands and face spoke more and more;
Her legs took her to a freedom she had never felt before.

Hannah danced to the music's end, she held her pose and waited -
Her Ballet Teacher smiled at her from in the wings, elated!
She motioned for Hannah to walk downstage to take her bow...and THEN -
The audience was on the feet! They cheered and cheered again!!
Hannah received her flowers, and through happy tears she bowed,
Then walked offstage with Ballet Teacher, higher than the clouds!

Hannah had danced her heart out, and though no other sound was heard,
She said all that she had to say yet never spoke a word.
Her gift to all was silent, and though she never had to speak,
Hannah found her voice that day; her life was now complete.

The End

About the Author:

Robin Conrad Sturm began her ballet training at seven and a half years of age with Mary Day, and went on to become a graduate of the Academy of the Washington School of the Ballet. She was a full-scholarship student at the American Ballet Theatre School and the School of American Ballet in New York. She was a founding member of the Washington Ballet. Ms. Sturm and her husband, Bob, have three grown children, Jeremy, Rebekah, and Samantha. They live in Manassas, Virginia, where they co-direct the Asaph Dance Ensemble.

Made in the USA
Middletown, DE
07 February 2019